Double Trouble

Adapted by N.B. Grace

Based on the television series, "The Suite Life of Zack & Cody", created by Danny Kallis & Jim Geoghan

Based on the episode written by Danny Kallis & Jim Geoghan

New York

Printed in the United States of America

First Edition
1 3 5 7 9 10 8 6 4 2

Library of Congress Catalog Card Number on file.

ISBN 0-7868-4936-3

For more Disney Press fun, visit www.disneybooks.com
Visit DisneyChannel.com

Chapter 1

The lobby of the Tipton Hotel was bustling. Rich and famous guests were checking in, rich and famous guests were checking out, and hotel employees were running around taking care of them all. As usual, Mr. Moseby, the hotel manager, was stationed behind the front desk, keeping a careful eye on everything.

Two preppy teenage boys carrying sports-equipment bags entered the lobby. They dropped the bags against the front desk, startling Mr. Moseby.

"Hey, man," one of the boys said to Mr. Moseby.

"Yo, dudes," Mr. Moseby replied with a big smile, doing his best to sound hip.

But Mr. Moseby had a long way to go before he could ever be considered hip. He was wearing an elegant gray suit and a spotless tie. He simply did not look like someone who would use the word "dudes."

The two boys looked at each other, then shrugged. As long as Mr. Moseby could check them into their rooms, who cared what he called them?

Across the lobby, London Tipton, the daughter of the hotel's wealthy owner, was leaning against the candy counter. She was busy congratulating herself on the superfashionable outfit she had thrown together that morning: a gray fedora hat, a black-and-silver tank top, a short skirt, and pink pearls.

And now that she had spotted the two new hotel guests, she was even happier about her outfit.

"Mmm-mmm," she said to Cody and Zack Martin, the twelve-year-old twins who were manning the candy counter. "Look what the hunk fairy just dropped off. Jason Harrington and Kyle Lawford." She snapped her fingers at Zack and Cody. "Gloss me!" she commanded.

"Sorry, we're watching the counter for Maddie," Zack said. "And we're not allowed to accept money, make change, or touch any of the merchandise." *Especially* not the lip gloss, he thought with disdain.

"Is there anything you *can* do?" she pouted.

"I can shove twelve gummy worms up my nose," Cody said brightly. "Wanna see?"

London made a face just as Maddie Fitzpatrick, a hotel employee, breezed into the lobby, wearing a miniskirt, a green sweater, a pink-striped blouse, and boots. She looks nice enough, London thought to herself, but not as stylish as me—not by a long shot!

"Where have you been?" London barked. "Never mind." She snapped her fingers. "Gloss me, candy girl."

Maddie snapped her fingers back. "Off the clock," she said easily. London could be difficult, but Maddie knew how to handle her. Maddie smiled at Zack and Cody. "Thanks, guys."

"No problem, sweet thang," Zack said. He had heard an actor use the line on a late-night TV show, and the girl he had used it on had fallen in love with him by the first commercial break. Zack had memorized the line and practiced using it for a moment just like this.

But Maddie said, very nicely, "Awww. Call me in ten years."

Zack's face fell. Apparently, flirting is harder than it looks on TV, he thought to himself.

Maddie checked her watch. "If I hurry, I can make family night at Buffet Town," she said, adding, "it's my turn to pretend it's my birthday."

London sighed. For some reason, Maddie seemed to like chain restaurants and special menu deals. It was so *not rich* of her!

Speaking of rich . . . London thought, as Kyle and Jason walked toward her.

"London?" Kyle asked. "Hey, London!"

"Kyle! Small world," she said as casually as she could.

Jason was staring at Maddie, clearly smitten. "Hi," he said to her. "I'm Jason."

Maddie stared back. "I'm . . . uh . . . uh . . ." she started.

"Maddie," Cody said helpfully.

Maddie nodded, still staring into Jason's gorgeous eyes. "What he said," she said.

"You come to the Tipton Hotel often?" Jason asked.

Maddie blinked. Jason must have thought she was a hotel guest. As if she would ever have enough money to pay for a room at the Tipton!

Still, she thought, why not play along? She nodded. "Constantly. It's like I live here." Which, she thought, wasn't *exactly* a lie. . . . She did work really long hours.

Well, this is cute, London thought, as she

watched Maddie fall head over heels right in front of her. But let's get the focus back on *me*! "So, Kyle," she said, batting her eyes. "You in town for the Usher concert?"

"Semester break," Kyle explained. "Our parents arrive from Aspen tomorrow. Then we fly to Bermuda." He shrugged. "Our moms lost their tans skiing."

Maddie's eyes widened at the thought of flying to Bermuda after a ski vacation just so you could get your tan back. "Oh, I hate when that happens," she said.

Maddie checked her watch again. "Well, as we say, gotta jet," she said. She turned to Jason and smiled. "Nice to meet you."

As Maddie walked toward the door, Zack ran after her. "You don't really like that guy, do you?" he asked.

Maddie glanced back at Jason and shrugged. "He's cute," she admitted, "but

I've worked here long enough to know his type. Rich people don't care about anything but themselves."

They both watched as Kyle started to throw his soda can into the garbage. Jason grabbed the can from him and said, "Whoa, hey, man, recycle that!"

"Are you serious?" Kyle asked.

Maddie ran back toward Jason. "You recycle?" she asked.

"Sure," Jason nodded. "Cans, bottles, newspapers."

Maddie's eyes narrowed. Was he for real, she wondered, or just trying to make himself look good? "Since when?" she asked.

Jason laughed a little. "Since my father bought Oregon and started chopping down the trees," he admitted. "Have you heard of Opticorp?"

Maddie gasped. "The center of all evil?"

"That's Dad," Jason said ruefully.

Maddie couldn't believe it. "I protested against them!" she told Jason.

"Me, too!" he said excitedly.

"I got dragged off by a cop!" Maddie added.

"I got grounded for two weeks!" Jason countered.

Hmmm, London thought. Sparks really seem to fly when people talk about recycling. Well, she had never been much of an eco-freak, but it might be worth a try. . . .

She turned to Kyle. "I recycle, too."

"Really?" Kyle looked doubtful.

London nodded eagerly and twirled the strands of her pink pearl necklace. "I wore these pearls yesterday!" she explained.

Kyle smiled. London may not really understand the concept of recycling, he thought, but she's a lot of fun.

Chapter 2

The next morning, Kyle and Jason took the elevator down to the lobby where London was waiting eagerly. "Hi, Kyle! Jason!" she called, waving at them. "I got us tickets to Usher! Front row! So close he'll probably sweat on us!"

"Awesome!" Kyle answered.

"Excuse me," Jason said as he left to greet

Maddie, who had just entered the hotel, still dressed in her regular clothes. "Hey, Maddie," he said.

"Hi," Maddie said.

London watched Jason go, a little puzzled. "What is that all about?"

Kyle laughed as he watched his friend. "She's all he could talk about last night," he explained.

London rolled her eyes. "Oh, please. They are sooo not right for each other."

"I don't know," Kyle shrugged. How much did a guy and a girl need to have in common, anyway? "They're both rich," he offered.

"What?" London stared at Kyle, then at Jason and Maddie. The light dawned. "Oh, he thought—" She laughed. "I don't want to burst any bubbles, but it's so much fun."

She started walking toward Jason to explain all about Maddie and her part-time job. But before she could say anything, Mr. Moseby pulled her aside and said quietly, "London, a word. I couldn't help overhearing your plans—"

London beamed. Mr. Moseby was trying to make sure the night was absolutely perfect! Really, he was so helpful. She would have to tell her father to give him a raise.

"Oh, good," she said happily. "Then you'll have the hotel limo ready by eight o'clock?"

Mr. Moseby cleared his throat in embarrassment. "Love to, except your father saw this—" He held up a copy of a tabloid newspaper called *The National Inquiry*. A big photo of London was splashed across the front page, under a headline that read, LONDON'S WILD NIGHT.

Mr. Moseby shook his head at the thought of her father's reaction. "And he memoed me, 'No more of these.'"

"But, but . . ." she sputtered.

"No buts," Mr. Moseby said firmly. "It is unseemly that a girl your age be out alone with two boys."

London's mind was whirling. After all that work getting those concert tickets—true, she only had to call her father's assistant and ask for them, but still! It wasn't fair.

"But, um, um . . ." She glanced wildly around the room, trying to think of some way to get around her father's orders, and she saw Maddie. And Jason. Talking together and looking quite friendly. Hmm . . .

"I'm not going alone!" she said triumphantly. "Maddie's coming."

Mr. Moseby looked over at Maddie. She

was a nice young girl, he thought, perhaps even a little *too* straitlaced—the exact opposite of London, in fact.

As London watched Mr. Moseby's face, she could tell that he was weakening. She moved in for the kill.

"Nobody's going to have any real fun with Maddie around," she argued.

Mr. Moseby nodded. "Good point."

London smiled and went over to where Maddie was chatting with Jason. "Excuse me," London said, as she pulled Maddie to one side.

"What are you doing?" Maddie asked, annoyed that London had pulled her away from Jason.

"I'm inviting you to see Usher with me, Kyle, and Jason," London explained quickly.

Maddie eyed her suspiciously. It wasn't

like London to invite her anywhere. "Why?" she asked bluntly.

London rolled her eyes as if the answer was obvious. "Because I'm nice, duh," she said.

Maddie's eyes narrowed even more. It *really* wasn't like London to do something nice.

After a moment, London crumbled. "Okay, Moseby won't let me go unless I bring along a guaranteed killjoy," she snapped. Hmmm, she thought, that didn't come out quite right. . . . More brightly, she added, "So, what do you say?"

"As heartfelt as that offer is, no," Maddie said drily.

"Come on, Kyle says Jason likes you," London pleaded.

"Really?" Maddie glanced at Jason, her heart beating a little faster. It would be so awesome if he *did* like her, especially because she could feel herself falling for him. . . .

Then she caught herself. Time for a reality check, Maddie, she scolded herself. She said to London, "Rich guys don't date poor girls. Why would Jason want to go out with me?"

London thought fast. "Well, you're smart and cute," she said. Maddie smiled, and London decided her smooth talk was working. "He obviously doesn't mind girls with big feet," she added.

Maddie's face fell, but London didn't notice. "Oh, and he thinks you're rich," she said quickly, hoping that would slide right past Maddie.

No such luck. Maddie looked really disappointed. Just as she had thought—rich boys only wanted to date rich girls. "No wonder he's paying attention to me," she said. Then she straightened her shoulders and said, "I'll go set him straight."

"No, just play along," London urged, trying to stay calm. If she couldn't convince Maddie to go on this double date, her whole evening was ruined! "Please. It's only for one night." She lowered her voice as she told Maddie what she would miss if she didn't go. "Front-row seats. Backstage passes. You get to ride in a limo that's not following a hearse. . . ."

Maddie smiled as she imagined the evening. All she had to do was pretend to be something she wasn't for a few more hours!

"We get to meet Usher?" Maddie asked hopefully.

London gave her a look. "Sweetie, Usher gets to meet *us*," she bragged.

Who could resist such an invitation?

Not me, Maddie thought. "Just call me Princess," she said happily.

Later—much later—that night, Maddie, London, Kyle, and Jason returned to the hotel, carrying the T-shirts, posters, and CDs they had been given at the concert. The elevator doors opened on the floor where Zack, Cody, and their mom lived.

Maddie danced out of the elevator. "This whole night has been so awesome!" she gushed. She held up the badge that was hanging around her neck. The passes had gotten them backstage, where they hung out with celebrities after the concert. "Look, I'm a VIP!"

Jason smiled at her. "You know, you're amazing," he said. "It's like it's all new to you. Front-row seats, meeting celebrities, riding in limos . . ."

Oops! Maddie suddenly realized that she had been acting *way* too excited. A rich girl would be used to this kind of treatment; she wouldn't get all keyed up about chatting with Usher or getting a free T-shirt. Quickly, she said, "Well, I never get tired of sticking my head out the sunroof and yelling, 'Woo!'"

Inside the suite, Zack and Cody were putting some stuff away when they heard a strange sound from the hall. Cody looked at Zack and asked, "Did you hear someone go 'woo'?"

"It must be Maddie." Zack motioned to Cody to kneel in front of the door and said, "Get down."

What was Zack up to now? Cody shrugged; if there was one thing he knew about his brother, it was that he always had a plan. . . .

London had a plan, too. As they all stood in the hallway, she suddenly said, "Let's all go to the rooftop!" She added quickly, "Except for Jason and Maddie."

Kyle grinned as he and London got back on the elevator and headed to the roof.

Jason smiled, too. Finally, he and Maddie were alone together. He put his arm around her. "So I guess I should say good night," he said, adding, "or you could invite me into your suite."

"My sweet what?" Maddie asked blankly. Being this close to Jason seemed to make her mind all fuzzy . . . then she snapped to. "Oh, my *suite*," she said, suddenly understanding. "In the hotel. Where I live. Because I'm rich." She had to get out of this, and fast. "No, you can't come in."

Good move, Maddie, Zack thought, as he stood on Cody's back and watched through the peephole. "I think that creep's trying to kiss her!" he said, outraged. "Man, if I was five years older and two feet taller—"

"I'd be squashed," Cody interrupted, sounding a little disgruntled. How much longer was Zack going to spy on Maddie? Cody was *already* feeling a little squashed. He could hear Maddie's voice very faintly through the door, and he sighed with relief. It sounded as if she was wrapping things up. . . .

"So, you're leaving tomorrow?" Maddie was asking. "Well I guess we should—"

"Should start kissing now?" Jason interrupted. He smiled at her.

Whoa! Maddie blinked. "But I hardly know you," she said.

"Right, so a good-bye kiss," he pointed out.

"Yes," Maddie smiled, adding quickly, "bye."

"Bye," Jason said, just as quickly. Then he bent down to kiss her. . . .

Thud! A muffled crash and voices came from inside the suite, where Zack and Cody had fallen down.

Jason looked at Maddie. "What was that?"

Maddie had her suspicions, but she wasn't about to reveal them.

"Cats?" she suggested. "Big cats?"

Jason looked at her skeptically. She sighed and said, "Actually, they're the hotel singer's twins." He's going to ask why they're in my room, she thought. Good question. If only I had a good answer. . . . She thought fast and added, "When she works late, I let them stay with me."

He gazed at her with admiration. "You are so amaz—" he began.

"Yes, I am," Maddie interrupted. It was so nice to have Jason looking at her like that. Too bad, she thought gloomily, the look was based on a complete and total lie. "Well, I better go."

She turned to open the door, but Jason stopped her. "Not before you say good-bye," he said.

Maddie looked up into his eyes and felt herself melting. What did one little lie matter? He was leaving tomorrow and she'd never see him again. And he was so cute. . . . She leaned in and they kissed.

Inside the suite, now Cody was standing on Zack's back spying through the peephole. "They're kissing good-bye," Cody said with a giggle.

"Didn't they just say good-bye?" Zack asked grumpily.

Chapter 3

The next morning, Carey Martin, Zack and Cody's mom, bustled around the suite fixing breakfast. Maddie emerged from the bathroom, ready to face the day.

"Thanks for letting me stay the night," she said to Carey. By the time she and Jason finished saying good-bye, it was two A.M., so Zack and Cody's mother had invited Maddie to bunk there.

Carey put a plate of pancakes on the table and said to Maddie, "You know, word on the street is Jason's kinda cute."

Maddie grinned. "Beyond," she agreed, ignoring Zack's sudden scowl. She went on, "And he thinks I'm the most intelligent, beautiful, down-to-earth rich girl he's ever met."

"Okay, okay, whoa!" Carey frowned slightly. "Back up. *Rich*?"

Maddie sighed. She should have known she couldn't slip anything past Zack and Cody's mom. "It's complicated," she said. "I was doing London a favor. It's not like I wanted to do it."

"Oh, yeah, it must have been torture to have to kiss that boy," Carey agreed drily. Maddie gave her a startled look, and she added, "The cats told me."

Maddie glared at Zack and Cody, who

suddenly became very interested in eating their breakfast.

"When are you going to tell him the truth?" Carey asked. She had a knack, Maddie thought, for asking uncomfortable questions.

"Never," Maddie said. "He's gone. It was only for one night, and I'll never see him again."

Before Zack and Cody's mother could continue the conversation, her twin sons got up and headed for the door, their breakfast finished.

"Maddie, will you take us to the park on your way home?" Zack asked eagerly.

"Sure," Maddie said good-naturedly. "Come on."

As they headed out the door, Carey warned her sons, "And don't bring back another homeless squirrel."

"Awww," Zack and Cody groaned in unison.

As their mother gave them her sternest I'm-the-mom-and-I-mean-it look, the phone rang. While Zack answered it, Maddie and Cody went into the hall. Maddie was shocked to see Jason—and his parents!

"Oh, no," she said, before she could help herself. She tried to hide behind Cody, but it didn't work. He was just too short. And the hallway was just too narrow.

"Maddie!" Jason said happily. "These are my parents."

She nodded hello. "Hi, hi," Maddie said to them. "I, uh, thought you would be on your way to Bermuda by now."

"So did we," Mr. Herrington chuckled. "But Jason insisted on another night in Boston." He winked at her. "And now I know why."

"Yes, he's spoken of nothing else but you from the lobby up to our room," Jason's mother added. "And our room is on a very high floor."

Jason spotted Maddie's overnight bag. "You checking out?" he asked, disappointed.

"Uh, uh—" Maddie grasped for something to say.

Fortunately, Cody rescued her. "No, she's moving to the top floor," he said, adding in an impressive voice, "The Imperial Suite. Her old suite—" He nodded toward the door of the suite they had just left. "—was the wrong shade of beige."

Jason and his parents nodded as if this excuse made perfect sense. I guess if you live in the Land of the Rich, Maddie thought, you don't think twice about demanding a better room because the paint on the walls isn't quite to your liking. Yet another reason why I will never fit in with Jason and his family.

"We were just coming down to invite you to dinner," Jason said. "I convinced them to take us to Club Nouveau."

"Really?" Maddie said. Club Nouveau! She had heard about it, of course, but she never thought she would get to go there!

Then her good mood disappeared. You're a fake, she reminded herself. This charade has got to stop!

"Wow . . . I can't go," she added, sounding truly disappointed. She tried to come up with a good excuse. "I promised I'd babysit the boys tonight."

Jason's mother smiled at her. "Yes, Jason told us about your charity work with indigent children," she said.

Indigent? Maddie thought angrily. That's going a bit far. Zack and Cody aren't poor.

They're just not rich. And neither am I.

At that moment, Zack bounded into the hall. "Hey, Cody, Josh called," he said. "We're sleeping over at his house tonight."

Jason and his parents turned to Maddie and beamed.

"Excellent," his father said. "Now you can join us."

"Uh," Maddie said. Now she had no choice.

"We're on the top floor as well," he continued. "In fact, we'll pick you up. Seven o'clock, sharp."

Maddie nodded weakly. I'm doomed, she thought. Totally doomed.

This is how big trouble starts, Maddie thought. With just one little lie.

She was sitting with Zack and Cody in their suite, trying to figure out how she was going to make it look like she was staying in the hotel's nicest suite.

"What am I going to do?" she wailed.

"Well, here's a wild thought," Cody said. "Tell him the truth."

"I don't think so," Maddie said. "If I tell them now, Jason will look like a fool, and I'll look like, like—"

"A lying gold digger?" Cody suggested. Maddie glared at him, and he added hastily, "Which you're not."

"How am I gonna get out of this?" she moaned.

"We'll help you with Jason," Cody said confidently.

Zack stared at him in disbelief. "Why would I help my future wife hook up with some other dude?"

"'Cause he's leaving tomorrow," Cody explained patiently, "and she'll owe you big-time."

Zack nodded. Cody had a point. A very good point.

"Okay, here's what we do," he said briskly. "First, we get you an Imperial Suite."

Maddie sighed. "Do you have any idea how much they cost?"

Cody smiled at his brother, an isn't-she-funny kind of smile. "Awww," he said, "she thought we were gonna *pay*."

Zack smiled back, an I-know-she's-so-cute-that-way kind of smile. "That's sweet." Then he turned to Maddie and, imitating that TV actor who was so good at flirting, he said, "No, we don't pay, baby."

A few moments later, they had a plan. They took the elevator to the lobby, ready to put it into action.

Cody strolled by the front desk casually. Just as he walked in front of the clerk, he pretended to trip and fall.

"Oh, no!" he yelled. "I think I hurt my coccyx."

The clerk rushed from behind the counter to help Cody, his face creased with worry. The last thing the Tipton Hotel needed was a lawsuit, he thought to himself.

As the clerk checked Cody for injuries, Zack dashed to the front desk from his hiding place behind a potted plant. He grabbed a key card, swiped it in the computer, and dashed away again.

Cody was still lying on the ground, clutching his back, but he had seen his brother escape. He smiled up at the clerk. "All better now," he beamed. "Thank you."

He bounced up and ran after Zack, who handed the key card to Maddie with a flourish. She took it, reluctantly admiring their derring-do, and said, "But I don't have anything to wear to Club Nouveau."

"Please," Zack scoffed. "Give us a challenge."

❖❖❖

A short time later, Zack and Cody lurked in the hallway outside the Imperial Suite. Since they lived at the hotel, they knew everyone's regular routines: the bellboys', the maids', Mr. Moseby's. In fact, they made it their business to know. You never knew when that kind of information would come in handy. Like now.

Zack and Cody watched as Esteban, the bellboy, stepped off the elevator and started walking down the hall, carrying a beautiful dress wrapped in plastic.

Cody and Zack stepped in front of him, a look of urgency on their faces.

"Esteban!" Cody said. "Mr. Moseby's yelling for you."

Esteban immediately looked nervous, as Zack and Cody had known he would. Esteban lived to please Mr. Moseby—which was *not* an easy task.

"For me?" Esteban said anxiously. "He never yells *for* me. He yells *at* me." Then he smiled and added, "But only when I deserve it, which is often." He became serious again. "He is a great man."

"Well, you're keeping a great man waiting," Zack said briskly. It was time to move their plan along.

"Oh, but this dress must go to London," Esteban said.

"We'll take it," Cody said.

"Bless you, little blond people," Esteban

said as he handed the dress to the twins and rushed back to the elevator.

A few hours later, Maddie stood in front of Zack and Cody in the Imperial Suite. The suite was amazing. It had thick gold curtains, a glittering chandelier, plush furniture, and vases of flowers everywhere.

And Maddie looked like she belonged there. She was wearing London's designer gown. Her hair was pulled back elegantly, and she had on a necklace and earrings Zack and Cody had "borrowed" from their mother. She looked beautiful, glamorous, and very nervous.

The doorbell rang. Maddie jumped.

"How do I look?" she asked.

"Rich," Zack said.

"Good," she replied.

Cody and Zack marched to the suite's double door and opened it with a bow.

"Enter," Zack said grandly.

Jason's mother smiled at them blandly. "Oh, look, you've put the little inner-city boys to work," she said. "They're so cute." She turned to one side and whispered to Maddie, "Be sure to check their pockets before they leave."

Before Maddie could respond, Jason's father strolled across the room to look out the floor-to-ceiling windows. "Fabulous view," he commented. "You can see the park from here."

Jason couldn't resist a little dig. "Yes," he replied, "that's what trees look like before you cut them down."

"Our little rebel," his mother said fondly.

Jason's father forced a laugh. "My son

doesn't approve of what I do," he explained to Maddie. With an edge to his voice, he added, "even though it pays for everything *he* does."

Oh, dear, Maddie thought. All I need is more tension tonight!

"*I* know," Jason's mother said lightly, clearly trying to keep the peace. "Why don't we come back here after the dinner that *George* pays for and look at the trees that *Jason* loves and have dessert?"

Her husband looked at her. Hurriedly, Maddie said, "Shouldn't we be heading out? I hear Club Nouveau is off the hook."

But Jason's mother, unfortunately, had other ideas. "Actually, all the Boston papers say the hottest ticket in town is right here at the Hotel Tipton," she said. "It's Carey Martin, the indigents' mother."

Maddie felt her stomach turn to ice.

Please, she thought, don't suggest that we go downstairs to the cabaret—

"She's great!" Cody said. He was always his mother's biggest fan, next to Zack, of course. "If you only have one night here, you gotta see her."

Maddie gritted her teeth. Cody was so excited about his mother's show, he had forgotten the evening's goal: to make sure that no one found out that Maddie was the candy-counter girl. "Although I'm sure we could find someone just as good, who is *not* at this hotel," she said, as sweetly as possible.

"Nonsense," George said firmly. "We have reservations."

"So do I," Maddie said weakly as she followed them out of the suite.

Chapter 4

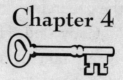

Zack and Cody walked Jason, his parents, and Maddie downstairs to the cabaret where their mother was singing. Esteban the bellboy noticed Maddie's dress as they passed and looked confused for a moment. Cody quickly called out, "Keep on movin', folks!" and the group swept by before Esteban could say anything.

As they approached the cabaret, Zack looked around and called out to a waiter, "Only the best table for my friends!"

"I don't want your mom to see us!" Maddie whispered urgently.

Zack nodded and, without missing a beat, added, "Which is way in the back, behind a pole!"

He gestured toward the table that was farthest from the stage. As Maddie and the Herringtons headed in that direction, Cody turned to Zack and said smugly, "We are good."

Zack grinned and the twins did their special handshake, complete with dance steps.

Just as they were finishing their celebration, a very large, very muscular man with short hair and an intimidating expression walked through the front door.

Mr. Moseby snapped to attention as he recognized The Amputator, a world-famous wrestler who often stayed at the hotel.

"Mr. Amputator, a pleasure to see you again!" he said. "Another Wrestle Royale at the Garden?"

The Amputator nodded and greeted him. "Moseby."

Zack's eyes lit up as he turned to Cody. "The Amputator's here! He's my favorite wrestler!"

"Your Imperial Suite awaits," Mr. Moseby announced grandly.

The Amputator looked pleased.

Cody looked horrified.

"And he's staying in Maddie's suite!" he gasped.

Zack and Cody exchanged dismayed glances as they overheard The Amputator ask Moseby, "Is that the expensive one?"

"Everything at the Tipton is expensive," Mr. Moseby assured him.

The Amputator nodded, pleased. "Perfect," he said. "The promoter's paying for it."

Mr. Moseby nodded understandingly. "We'll stick it to him good," he assured the wrestler.

Cody turned to his brother. "What do we do now? We've got to get him out of that room before Maddie gets back."

"Just stall him," Zack said. "When I'm done with that room, he's gonna wish he had never checked in." He pulled out his trusty multitool, smiled mischievously, and headed for the elevator.

Cody watched as Mr. Moseby pretended to reach for The Amputator's luggage, saying, "Need a hand lifting that?" He laughed at his own joke as The Amputator lifted both bags easily and added, "Just kidding, just kidding."

As Mr. Moseby started to lead the star

wrestler toward the elevator, Cody intercepted them. He didn't know how he was going to stall them, but he knew he had to give his brother time to do whatever it was that Zack planned to do.

"Excuse me," he said. "Mr. Amputator, I don't mean to bother you, but I'm a big fan. Could I have your autograph?"

The wrestler smiled. He loved meeting his fans—especially his young fans, who still had so much to learn about the fine art of putting people in headlocks and slamming them to the ground. "Well, of course you can, young man," he said.

He pulled out a pen as Mr. Moseby sighed with impatience.

Maybe I can stretch this moment out just a little bit longer, Cody thought. He said, "Could you write, 'To Cody . . . a young man I have just met'—that's M-E-T."

The Amputator looked at him coolly to show that he didn't need the spelling lesson. Mr. Moseby started tapping his foot.

Cody continued with his suggested wording. "'And yet, I feel I've known you for a long, long, long, time and . . .'"

As Cody went on and on, The Amputator sighed loudly. So did Mr. Moseby.

Upstairs in the Imperial Suite, Zack dashed around the room, gathering up all of Maddie's clothes. After looking frantically for a place to hide them, he decided to take the easy way out—and tossed them out the window.

Then he pulled his multitool from his pocket, dived under the coffee table, and began to unscrew the legs.

The first part of his plan was underway.

Maddie's clothes drifted to the ground outside the lobby windows, but no one noticed. The Amputator was too busy writing, Mr. Moseby was too busy trying to quell his irritation, and Cody was too busy suggesting even more additions to the note The Amputator was writing.

". . . long . . . long . . . long . . ." Cody said.

Finally, Mr. Moseby snapped. "Is there no end to this novel?" He turned to The Amputator. "My apologies."

The Amputator waved him off, and handed Cody the note. "Don't worry. I put, 'To Cody, Love, The Amputator.' How's that?"

"That's cool," Cody said as he took the note. The wrestler started toward the elevator and Cody followed, determined to keep the conversation going. He didn't know how

"Gloss me," London commanded.

"Just call me Princess," Maddie said happily.

"He's gone. It was only for one night, and I'll never see him again," Maddie said.

"We'll help you with Jason," Cody said.

"How do I look?" Maddie asked.

"I'm tellin' the truth, your dress was eaten by
wild Argentinian moths," Zack said.

"All right," Zack said, "let's put this puppy
back together."

"I just thought you were like all of the other
rich guys I've met," Maddie said.

much time he had been able to give Zack, but he had a feeling it wasn't enough.

"You know, most celebrities wouldn't take the time out to talk to a kid like me," he said chattily. "But you, you're different. What floor you staying on? Five? Twelve? Fourteen? Seventeen? Twenty? Basement?" As he called out each number, he helpfully punched the corresponding buttons.

"Well, actually, it's twenty-five," The Amputator said drily. "But thanks for hittin' all the buttons for me."

Cody nodded cheerfully and left the elevator before it started its long, slow trip to the top floor.

Always glad to be of service, he thought. Now it was time to warn Zack. . . .

Zack was busy behind the sofa when the phone in the Imperial Suite rang. He popped up, wondering for a moment if he should answer it. Finally, he did, careful to disguise his identity by saying "hello" in as deep a voice as possible.

"Get out, now!" Cody snapped. "I'm warning Maddie." Quickly, he hung up and ran off toward the cabaret.

As Cody entered the cabaret room, he tried to get Maddie's attention. "Psst!" Cody whispered. "Maddie. Maddie!"

It was no use. Maddie didn't hear him— but a couple sitting at a nearby table did, and shot him a dirty look.

From the stage, where she was in the middle of a set, Cody's mother noticed the annoyed couple. Distracted, she looked to see what had bothered them—and was puzzled to see Cody duck down and start crawling between the tables.

What is that boy up to now? Carey wondered, even as she continued smiling and singing. Casually, she moved along the stage, trying to keep Cody in sight.

There he was, creeping past that table with the newly engaged couple. . . . Now she had lost him. She craned her neck, trying to see over the table on the left—no luck. She bent down low and craned her neck to one side . . . was that Cody's sneaker under the tablecloth?

At the Herrington's table, Jason's father looked confused. "Does she always move like that?" he whispered to Maddie as he watched Carey's contortions.

Maddie whispered back, "No, normally she—" Suddenly, she felt a hand grab her ankle! She jumped in her seat and let out a little scream.

Onstage, Carey had heard Maddie yelp. Now she knew *exactly* where Cody was.

Jason and his parents looked at Maddie,

startled by her strange reaction. She smiled back weakly and said, "Excuse me. I dropped my fork."

Quickly, she knocked her fork on the ground and ducked under the table, where she found Cody waiting.

"What are you doing here?" she whispered, irritated.

"Moseby rented your suite to The Amputator," he explained.

"Really?" Maddie said in delight. "I love him."

Cody rolled his eyes in exasperation. "Hel-lo," he said. "Big picture. We're getting him out." He handed her his cell phone. "Here. I'll call you when the coast is clear."

Jason called down to Maddie. "You okay?

She popped back up, all smiles. "Great," she lied.

Carey was staring directly at Maddie with

an I-mean-business look on her face. Maddie gulped and slid a little lower in her seat. Somehow, she knew that she was going to have to answer some questions in the near future—and she also knew it wasn't going to be pretty.

Chapter 5

Inside the Imperial Suite, Zack had just removed a six-inch length of pipe from the bathroom plumbing when he heard a key turn in the lock.

He darted to one side of the door. As it opened, he tossed a spare coin on the floor.

The Amputator entered and immediately spotted the coin. "Ooh, a quarter!" he said, leaning over to pick it up.

That was the moment Zack had been waiting for. He dashed into the hall and slammed the door shut. He was free and clear.

Or at least he would have been, if he hadn't run into London as she stormed around the corner.

"I've been looking for you!" she cried, her eyes flashing. "Esteban told me he gave you my Paris original. Where is it?"

Zack gulped. "Paris?" he suggested.

Inside the suite, The Amputator put his bag on the coffee table with a grunt. He was a lean, mean fighting machine, but even *he* didn't enjoy carrying his own luggage.

Crash! The table collapsed under the weight of the bag.

The Amputator stared at the mess. Hmmm, maybe the bag had been heavier than he'd thought.

❖❖❖

Outside the suite, Zack was facing a furious London. "I'm tellin' the truth, your dress was eaten by wild Argentinian moths," Zack said, a little desperately. He was doing his best, but even *he* didn't buy the story he was weaving.

"Get me my dress right now!" London demanded, just as Cody got off the elevator.

Zack sighed with relief at the sight of his brother. Finally, a little help had arrived.

"You told her we gave it to Maddie?" Cody asked his brother.

Zack glared at him. "Noooo," he said pointedly.

Too late, Cody caught on. "Good," he said, lamely trying to recover. "Because we didn't do that."

Interesting, Zack thought. He wouldn't have thought London could look any angrier—but apparently she could. . . .

Inside the suite, The Amputator grabbed a glass and headed to the bar. It had been a long flight, and he wanted some water.

He got even more than he bargained for when he turned on the faucet—water sprayed right at his face!

After one brief, startled moment, he shrugged and opened his mouth to take a nice long drink. No sense wasting it, after all.

London looked as if she was ready to call the police and have the twins hauled off to jail for stealing, lying, and generally messing up her life. Instead, she picked up the hall phone and said, "I'm telling Moseby right now."

Zack and Cody looked at each other, alarmed. Mr. Moseby was *worse* than the police! With one movement, they both reached out to hang up the phone, and Zack said, "We'll take you to Maddie. You win."

But Zack, of course, had a Plan B. As they led her down the hall, he stopped at a closet door, guessing that London never paid attention to minor details of hotel architecture.

"She's changing in here," he said with great sincerity.

London peeked in the door. "In here?"

As London leaned in, Zack pushed her into the closet and Cody wedged a chair under the doorknob.

"Hey!" London's voice was muffled, but they clearly heard her next, horrified comment. "I'm standing in a bucket!"

As she pounded on the door, the twins ran off down the hall.

Time to work on Plan C.

The Amputator was still damp, but he wanted to sit down for a minute. When he lowered himself into his chair, however, it collapsed beneath him and he tumbled onto the floor.

He eyed the coffee table, then nudged it with his toe. Just as he thought. The table also fell to pieces.

"Okay," he said to himself. "What else can go wrong?"

As if in answer, the lights flickered, then went out. The Amputator was completely in the dark.

There was another *thunk*, as if something had fallen, and The Amputator said, "Ow."

He decided not to say or do anything for a few minutes. He already had more bruises than he had gotten in last year's championship wrestling match. . . .

Finally, The Amputator pulled himself together and left the suite. Carrying his luggage, he walked down the hall, a fresh bandage on his head, his shoes squishing with every step.

Zack and Cody watched him from their spot by the fuse box, which they had just tripped in order to douse the lights in his suite. When they were sure he was gone, they darted through the door and stood in the middle of the room, surveying the damage.

"All right," Zack said, "let's put this puppy back together."

He whipped out his trusty minitool and they got to work.

Downstairs in the cabaret, Maddie was feeling extremely uncomfortable. Zack and Cody's mom had joined their table after finishing her set, and Jason's mother was talking about Maddie.

"You must be so grateful," Mrs. Herrington gushed. "I mean, how many young girls would let a struggling single mother with two children stay in her suite?"

Carey gave Maddie a dark look. However, she merely said, as sweetly as possible, "It's so much nicer than the minivan we used to live in."

"And wait until you see her new suite," Mrs. Herrington babbled.

Carey raised an eyebrow at Maddie. "I'd love to see your new suite," she said, even more pleasantly.

"No, you don't want to see my new suite," Maddie said, a bit desperately. She already felt guilty enough for lying to Jason!

She felt a little sick, as if she were trapped in a nightmare and couldn't escape. . . .

Her cell phone rang.

"Yeah?" Maddie said. She listened for a moment, then smiled with relief.

She turned to the others. "Okay, let's go see my new suite."

Cody hung up the phone in the Imperial Suite. "Okay, they're coming," he said to Zack, who was smoothing a pillow.

The suite now looked perfect, with no sign of the destruction it had recently suffered. The boys looked around with satisfaction.

"We are so good," Zack said.

"Is there a hall of fame for this kind of stuff?" Cody wondered.

"Yes. It's called prison." Mr. Moseby's voice came from behind them.

The boys whirled around, horrified to see Mr. Moseby and The Amputator standing in front of them.

"Mr. Moseby!" they yelled in unison.

The Amputator stared at the boys, his mouth open in shock. "There's two of 'em?" he asked Mr. Moseby.

The concierge sighed. "Except in my dreams, where I see them by the hundreds."

Before he could continue, Maddie entered the suite, followed closely by Mrs. Martin, Jason, and Jason's parents. She was smiling at the thought of showing them the suite—until she caught sight of Mr. Moseby, The Amputator, and the twins.

"Oh, boy," she said.

"What are all of these people doing in your suite?" Mr. Herrington asked.

Jason turned to Maddie. "Maddie, what's going on?"

Maddie gulped. How could she ever explain this? "What's going on is . . ."

Thankfully, she didn't have to finish that sentence, because at that moment London burst into the room, her foot still stuck in a bucket from the closet.

"Aha!" she cried. She stomped into the room and pointed accusingly at Maddie. "Get out of my dress!"

Jason looked back and forth between London and Maddie. "What does she mean, *her* dress?"

"She designed it," Zack suggested. It was a far-fetched idea, but worth a try. . . .

His mother grabbed his collar. "Let it go," she said sternly.

Maddie sighed. There was no way around it. She would just have to come clean. "She means it's not mine," she confessed. "I'm not rich. I work at the hotel as the candy-counter girl."

"I knew she wasn't rich," Mr. Herrington said. "She's too nice."

"I don't know what I was thinking," Maddie said. "I was pretending to be something that I'm not . . . and I'm sorry."

She ran out of the room, crying.

Why had she thought she could pull it off? She had messed everything up.

Chapter 6

Maddie stood in the elevator, still crying. As the doors began to close, Carey stopped them and stepped inside.

"Wait a second," Carey said.

"Look, I really don't feel like talking," Maddie said as the elevator began its descent.

Carey nodded. "Okay, I'll talk, you listen." She hugged Maddie. "Honey, you really shouldn't have lied to Jason in the first place."

"I know, but I just thought he wouldn't like me because we come from two separate worlds," Maddie admitted. "He comes from champagne and caviar and I come from beer and pretzels." She began to cry even harder.

At that moment, the elevator doors opened and a middle-aged Asian man stepped into the car.

"I'm sorry," Carey said to him. "Could you please take the next elevator?"

He smiled and nodded, but apparently didn't understand her request. The doors closed and the businessman watched, curious, as Maddie wailed, "I'm such a doofus. Now Jason will hate me."

"You don't know that," Carey replied. "And you're not giving yourself very much credit, either."

Maddie sobbed even harder. "I know," she cried. "I'm such a doofus."

"Stop saying that," Carey snapped. She turned to the businessman. "May I?"

Without waiting for a response, she whipped the handkerchief out of his suit pocket and handed it to Maddie. "Maddie, you shouldn't sell yourself short. I bet if you give Jason half a chance, he'll tell you the same thing."

"You think so?" Maddie sniffed.

"I know so," Carey said confidently.

Maddie blew her nose, then handed the handkerchief back to the businessman. Grimacing slightly, he waved it off. Maddie smiled. She was still a little teary-eyed, but she was beginning to feel better.

The next morning, the twins followed their mother across the lobby, complaining loudly.

"Mom, I can't believe you took away our TV," Zack said.

"Let's review, shall we?" his mom said briskly. "You destroyed the Imperial Suite, you almost ruined my show, you locked London in a closet, and you injured a professional wrestler."

"All to help a friend," Cody pointed out. The boys beamed proudly.

"And that should be its own reward," Carey replied.

The boys frowned. Somehow, the conversation hadn't gone quite the way they had planned. "Mom, come on," they said.

Across the lobby, Jason walked to the candy counter where Maddie stood on duty, wearing her uniform: a blue button-down shirt and a man's tie.

"Hi there," Jason said.

"Good morning, sir," Maddie said coolly.

"So this is the real you?" he asked.

"In all my blue-collar glory." Maddie hesitated, then dropped her professional pose. "Listen, Jason, I'm really sorry I didn't tell you the truth."

"So am I."

Maddie rushed on. "I just thought you were like all of the other rich guys I've met."

"You should have given me more credit than that," he replied.

"Sorry. I wasn't thinking." Maddie's tone was sincere.

"So we'll just say good-bye," he went on.

Her face fell. "Okay," she said, disappointed. "Good-bye."

He smiled a little. "You do remember what we do when we say good-bye?"

She smiled back, feeling happier. "I think so."

They leaned across the candy counter and kissed.

Very faintly, Maddie could hear Zack's outraged voice from across the lobby. "Again?" he cried. "How many times do they have to say good-bye?"

"Get over it," his brother advised wearily.

One night at the Tipton Hotel had been more action-packed than most of his wrestling matches, The Amputator thought as he checked out.

"I hope you enjoyed your stay here, Mr. Amputator," Mr. Moseby said.

"It was quite relaxing," The Amputator lied.

He glanced down at his leg, which Zack was holding in a death grip, then over his shoulder at Cody, who was clinging to his back.

"Say your prayers, Amputator!" Zack cried. "You are going down!"

"Thank you, Mr. Moseby," The Amputator said smoothly as he took back his credit card.

"The twin terrors have him in a sleeper hold!" Cody yelled, mimicking a wrestling announcer's voice.

The Amputator started across the lobby, unfazed by the boys' attempts to stop him— or at least slow him down.

Zack raised his eyebrows. "Apparently, not asleep yet," he said.

Hmmm. This wrestling business was harder than it looked, he thought. But maybe, with just a little more practice . . .

Don't miss the next story
about Zack and Cody!

Room of Doom

Adapted by M.C. King

Based on the television series, "The Suite Life of Zack & Cody", created by Danny Kallis & Jim Geoghan

Based on the episode written by Pamela Eels O'Connell

The room was a mess. On every surface, on every piece of furniture, lay a pile of something. There was a pile of dirty laundry, a pile of schoolbooks and papers, even a pile of pillows—although Zack and Cody Martin liked to think of that particular pile as a fort. The fluffy down pillows at the Tipton Hotel made the best pillow forts.

The Tipton was just about the fanciest hotel in Boston, and Zack and Cody were proud to call it home. Who wouldn't be? The Tipton had a rooftop pool with a Jacuzzi, a candy counter in the lobby, and a game room in the basement. There was twenty-four-hour room service, which meant ice cream anytime—not to mention cheeseburgers and turkey clubs. How had Zack and Cody gotten so lucky? Well, their mother, Carey, was a professional singer who'd been hired to perform regularly in the hotel ballroom. A rent-free suite on the twenty-third floor was one of the perks of the job.

Zack and Cody were twins. They were almost identical, but not quite. They each had blond hair and blue eyes, and they were around the same height. Really, it was their personalities that set them apart. Zack was the more fun-loving of the brothers; Cody, the more serious. Zack liked to think it was because he was so much older—in fact, he was ten whole minutes older!—that he was more willing to take a dare or play a prank. Zack liked to think he was the fearless brother.

Still, he had to admit he flinched when from inside the pillow fort he heard the suite door open, and the menacing sound of his mother's footsteps. She had a beautiful voice when it came to singing, but when it came to screaming, she was downright frightful. The pillows did nothing to muffle her high-pitched yell. "Guys, get out here!"

Zack didn't move. Instead, he remained motionless inside the pillow fort, while Cody—who'd been in the bedroom—emerged to confront her alone. "Yeah, Mom?" Zack heard Cody say in his most innocent voice.

Zack couldn't see, but he imagined his mother had her hands on her hips. And he didn't have to see her to hear the determination in her voice. "When I left, there was a room under this mess. I'd like it back. So start cleaning." He listened with relief as his mother left the room and Cody let out a bitter sigh.

"Great, next thing you know she's gonna make me take a bath," Zack heard his brother grumble. Then, an idea struck Zack, and he couldn't resist acting on it. He peered between the pillows to see Cody sorting through a pile of clothes. Then, with expert precision and speed, he reached his hand out and grabbed his unsuspecting brother's wrist in a death grip.

Cody shrieked, then scrambled back in terror, falling into a pile of dirty laundry.

"Gotcha!" Zack shouted triumphantly, busting out from the pillow fort.

Cody's eyes glazed over in fury, and he

grabbed Zack and wrestled him to the ground. "Got *you*!" he yelled back.

It was just then that their mother reentered. "Cody, why are you cleaning the carpet with your brother's face? Although, if it gets the stain out . . ."

Zack was thinking his plan worked brilliantly: not only had he scared the wits out of Cody, he'd gotten him in trouble, too! Only Cody turned it around. "Mommy," the younger twin whimpered, "Zack scared me again."

"Zack!" their mother scolded. "You know Cody is sensitive. Why do you try to scare him?"

"It's my job," Zack said, trying not to sound too smug about it.

"Well, you're fired," she told him. Exasperated, she left the two brothers to clean up their mess.

The Suite Life of Zack & Cody

Check out these other books based on *The Suite Life* of Zack & Cody!

PHOTOS FROM THE SHOW INSIDE!

4 pages of full-color photos inside!

Do Not Disturb

Available wherever books are sold!

Disney PRESS

Disney CHANNEL